For Matteo

Find out more about the Scaredy Cats at Shoo's fabulous website: www.shoo-rayner.co.uk

LINCOLNSHIRE COUNTY COUNCIL	
03918361	
PETERS	£3.99
23-Aug-05	JNRE

First paperback edition 2005
Copyright © Shoo Rayner 2005
The right of Shoo Rayner to be identified as the author
and illustrator of this work has been asserted by him in
accordance with the Copyright, Designs, and Patents Act, 1988.
A CIP catalogue record for this book is available
from the British Library.
ISBN 1 84362 444 3 (hardback)
ISBN 1 84362 733 7 (paperback)
1 3 5 7 9 10 8 6 4 2 (hardback)
1 3 5 7 9 10 8 6 4 2 (paperback)
Printed in Great Britain

Bluebeard's cat

Shoo Rayner

ORCHARD BOOKS

Max knew he was late. He'd been trapped in his owner's garage for hours. He had almost given up hope of rescue when the door creaked open. A towering shape stood in the doorway...

A deep voice boomed. "COME OUT, NOW!" A huge hand grabbed him, but somehow Max wriggled free.

He ran like the wind to the secret circle, and was soon explaining why he was late for the Secret Society of Scaredy Cats.

"I've always wanted to look in your garage," said Max's friend, Freddy. "What's it like?"

"Dark and scary!" said Max. "I wish I'd never gone in."

"Just because a door is open, it doesn't mean you should enter..." growled Kipling, their leader.

Silence fell upon the secret circle. Kipling's eyes narrowed into slits. He was ready to tell a story. The story they had all come to hear.

"This story is about Jade, an old friend of mine," Kipling began. "She was the most beautiful cat in the world."

Jade's owners were very proud of her. They took her to all the best cat shows, which she always won.

A strange man went to all the cat shows, too. He was named after his extraordinary blue beard.

Bluebeard was very rich. He collected
cats in a huge mansion full of locked
rooms. All the cats knew about him.
None of them wanted to be owned
by him because he seemed so odd.

Bluebeard adored beautiful Jade. But Jade's owners loved her and didn't want to sell her, so Bluebeard decided to steal Jade. Bluebeard knew that cats were curious creatures, so he hid a box in Jade's garden.

Jade just had to look inside it. She
was a cat. She couldn't help herself.

It was a trap! The next time Jade saw daylight, she was inside Bluebeard's mansion!

Jade blinked in the bright light.

"Oh my beauty!" sighed Bluebeard, picking Jade up and holding her to his beard.

Jade couldn't understand why no
one liked Bluebeard. He brushed and
groomed her, fed her the most tasty
food, and called her his darling.

Bluebeard opened all the doors in the house for her, so Jade was free to go anywhere she liked. She couldn't go outside, but so what? She had everything a cat could want indoors.

One door stayed firmly shut, though.
"You don't want to go in there, my
darling," Bluebeard whispered. "That's
where my other cats are. You're much
too special to mix with them."

Every day, as Jade wandered
through the house, she'd stop by the
closed door. She was lonely. She would
have liked some cat company.

One day, when she thought
Bluebeard was out, Jade pushed
against the door. She just had to see
if it would open. She was a cat. She
couldn't help herself.

The door clicked and opened up a
crack. Her little heart went skipetty-bip!

The door was heavy, but she pushed
and squeezed her way through.

Never would she have dreamed of the horror that met her eyes. Hundreds of display cases stood before her. They contained stuffed cats of every shape, colour, and kind. They stared with dead, glassy eyes.

She read the hand-written labels.
"Chang. Male. Breed: Burmese."

"Ruffles. Female. Breed: Maine Coone."

"Berty. Male. Breed: British Blue."

On a red velvet stand, one case stood alone and empty. Jade read the label.

Panic gripped her. This room was
to be her tomb! Then an angry voice
roared behind her. "You silly cat!"
Jade turned and froze.

Bluebeard filled the doorway. Rage swept across his face. "I was going to let you die of old age. You were special to me, now you've spoiled everything!"

He opened a drawer and removed a glinting surgeon's knife.

"You weren't supposed to know about my little hobby," he hissed. "Now everything has changed."

The knife flashed as he pointed
to the display cases.

"Taxidermy," he explained. "It's the art of stuffing animals. You, my little dear, were going to be the pride of my collection...you still will...only sooner than I thought!"

Bluebeard reached to close the door. Jade didn't wait. She bolted through the gap and screamed as the heavy door slammed on the tip of her tail, but she didn't stop.

Jade tore up the stairs. Seconds later,
Bluebeard followed, taking three steps
at a time.

"Come here, you little…" Bluebeard raged. "You can't get away. There's no escape!"

Up narrow, twisty stairs, Jade raced. In a tiny turret room, she saw a broken pane in the lattice window.

She squeezed through, onto the windowsill. The town swirled giddily below. A ledge ran around the outside of the turret. Nervously, Jade edged along it.

Bluebeard opened the window.

"Come back, Jade, my dear!" he called sweetly. "I didn't mean it. You're my little darling!"

Down in the street, a crowd gathered. Thinking Bluebeard was trying to save his cat, someone called the fire brigade.

Minutes later, a fireman was climbing a ladder to the top of the tower.

"Go away!" Bluebeard bellowed.

"It's OK," the fireman called, "I'll save your cat."

The fireman was inches away from Jade, who clung to the ledge, frozen with fear. Bluebeard leaned out and lunged at her.

His fingers clutched at her fur. She
felt her balance go. She closed her eyes
and fell...

...into the arms of the waiting fireman.

Triumphantly, the fireman turned to smile at Bluebeard, but he was too late...Bluebeard had reached out too far and now he was hurtling towards the street below...

The Scaredy Cats held their breath and stared at Kipling.

From far away they heard Max's owner's calling, "Max! Max! Come home! Where are you?"

"They sound worried," Kipling said to Max. "You'd better go. And remember, don't go looking in empty garages again. You know what they say? Curiosity killed the cat!"

SCAREDY CATS

Shoo Rayner

- ❏ Frankatstein   1 84362 729 9   £3.99
- ❏ Foggy Moggy Inn   1 84362 730 2   £3.99
- ❏ Catula   1 84362 731 0   £3.99
- ❏ Catkin Farm   1 84362 732 9   £3.99
- ❏ Bluebeard's Cat   1 84362 733 7   £3.99
- ❏ The Killer Catflap   1 84362 744 2   £3.99
- ❏ Dr Catkyll and Mr Hyde   1 84362 745 0   £3.99
- ❏ Catnapped   1 84362 746 9   £3.99

Little HORRORS

- ❏ The Swamp Man   1 84121 646 1   £3.99
- ❏ The Pumpkin Man   1 84121 644 5   £3.99
- ❏ The Spider Man   1 84121 648 8   £3.99
- ❏ The Sand Man   1 84121 650 X   £3.99
- ❏ The Shadow Man   1 84362 021 X   £3.99
- ❏ The Bone Man   1 84362 010 3   £3.99
- ❏ The Snow Man   1 84362 009 X   £3.99
- ❏ The Bogey Man   1 84362 011 1   £3.99

These books are available from all good bookshops,
or can be ordered direct from the publisher:
Orchard Books, PO BOX 29, Douglas IM99 1BQ
Credit card orders please telephone 01624 836000 or fax 01624 837033
or e-mail: bookshop@enterprise.net for details.

To order please quote title, author and ISBN and your full name and address.
Cheques and postal orders should be made payable to 'Bookpost plc'.
Postage and packing is FREE within the UK
(overseas customers should add £1.00 per book).

Prices and availability are subject to change.